CHAPTER 1

"A family tie is like a tree,

it can bend but it cannot break."

~ African proverb

PROLOGUE.
KONGO CITY...
MY NAME IS DR. ELIJAH BENJAMIN LATIMER III...
...OR, AS MY STUDENTS LIKE TO CALL ME... DR. TRE.
SPEAKING OF MY STUDENTS...
...A FEW MONTHS AGO, THREE OF THEM ACCIDENTALLY CAME INTO CONTACT WITH AN EXPERIMENT*
WHEN THREE TEENAGERS GAIN UNBELIEVABLE POWERS, THEY MUST LEARN TO BALANCE EXCITEMENT WITH RESPONSIBILITY AND FACE THE CHALLENGE OF BEING HEROES IN TODAY'S WORLD!
SWAG PATROL
IN CHAPTER ONE:
TRAINING DAY!
*SEE SWAG PATROL #0. AVAILABLE FOR FREE DOWNLOAD.

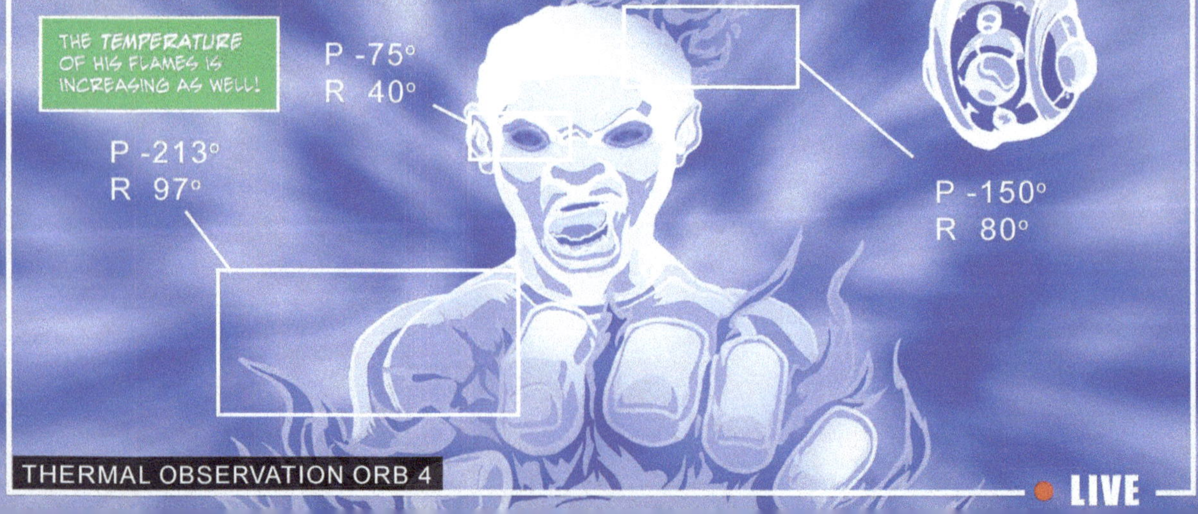

RASHAD CARTER. ...AGE 16.
HE CHOSE THE UNIQUE CODE NAME K-SWAG.
HE'S INCREDIBLY FAST AND I BELIEVE HE'S FAR FROM REACHING HIS TOP SPEED.
A.R.M
HR.
45
573 MPH
134°
HIS ABILITY TO GENERATE AND CONTROL FIRE IS IMPROVING TOO.
FWOOSH!
THE TEMPERATURE OF HIS FLAMES IS INCREASING AS WELL!
P -75°
R 40°
P -213°
R 97°
P -150°
R 80°
THERMAL OBSERVATION ORB 4
LIVE

THEN THERE'S HIS LITTLE SISTER, MYA CARTER, AKA: MINDSET. AGE 15.
THOOM!
THOOM!
THOOM!
OKAY.
...LET'S SEE IF I CAN TAKE THIS TO ANOTHER LEVEL!
HER FORCE FIELDS ARE STRONGER AND HOLD UP LONGER.
HER FLIGHT CAPABILITY IS ASTOUNDING.
SHE RECENTLY DEVELOPED A NEW POWER.
I THINK I'M GETTING THE HANG OF THIS!
...NOW, LET'S GIVE YOU A PIECE OF MY MIND!
IT'S IMPRESSIVE TO SAY THE LEAST.
BZZT!
BZZT!
BZZT!
SHE CAN CONVERT HER PSIONIC ENERGY INTO POWERFUL BLAST.

AND LASTLY THERE'S THEIR COUSIN CHRIS LOWERY. AGE 16.
YEAH! GET SOME!
KRAK!
HE PICKED THE NAME BLAZE.
UH-HUH!
HE HAS PHENOMENAL STRENGTH. SO FAR HE'S LIFTED TWO TONS WITH EASE.
HIS CONCUSSIVE ENERGY BLASTS ARE OFF THE CHARTS!
OH YEAH! THIS IS WHAT I CALL KICKING--
SHAKOOM!
BLAZE!? LANGUAGE.
AH? YEAH... SORRY, DR. TRE.
TOGETHER THEY CALL THEMSELVES SWAG PATROL AND WITH MY HELP...
...THEY WILL BECOME HEROES.
EVEN WITH INTENSE TRAINING AND IMPROVEMENTS OF THEIR ABILITIES...
NOT Ready
...I STILL DON'T BELIEVE THEY'RE READY FOR THE FIELD.
END PROLOGUE.

EXCELLENT TRAINING TODAY! YOU'RE GETTING STRONGER EVERY TIME.
THANKS DR. TRE!
HUFF. HUFF.
ONE OF OUR BEST SCORES YET!
COME ON DR. TRE, LET'S GO OUT THERE FOR ONCE!
BEEP! BEEP! BEEP!
EMERGENCY
WE CAN PUT OUR POWERS TO THE TEST.
NOT YET. YOU NEED JUST A LITTLE MORE TRAINING.
YOU'VE GOT TO BE KID- DING ME!
OH MAN! COME ON!
HMMM.
OKAY. SETTLE DOWN. YOU'RE NOT READY FOR A MISSION.
...BUT YOU ARE READY FOR SOMETHING ELSE...

CALL IT A REWARD FOR ALL YOUR HARD WORK.
"EACH SUIT IS MADE TO ACCOMPANY YOUR POWERS."
"THEY ALSO HAVE BUILT-IN TRACKING DEVICES AND COMMUNICATORS."
WOW!
THOSE SUITS ARE FIRE, DR TRE!
NOW THAT'S DOPE!
I'M GLAD YOU LIKE!
I HAVE TO GO TAKE CARE OF SOMETHING BUT I'LL SEE YOU TOMORROW. BE SURE TO LOCK UP WHEN YOU LEAVE.
BUZZ BUZZ
BUZZ BUZZ

JCI
J.C.I
JACKSON CONSOLIDATED, INC.
MR. JACKSON, WE GOT EYES ALL OVER THE CITY...
...NO ONE HAS SEEN THOSE KIDS IN MONTHS.
NO ONE KNOWS WHO THEY ARE. IF THEY WERE A THREAT, THEY WOULD'VE SHOWN UP BY NOW.
I DON'T PAY YOU FOR YOUR OPINIONS! STAY ALERT!
YES SIR.
THEY'LL RESURFACE EVENTUALLY.

MEANWHILE...
MARCUS GARVEY PARK.
YOU'RE SUPPOSE TO STAY IN TOUCH WITH A.R.M.*, DR. TRE!
YOU'VE BEEN IGNORING OUR CONTACTS FOR WEEKS.
APOLOGIES FOR NOT GETTING BACK SOONER. WORK HAS BEEN HECTIC!
SIR, HE'S DEFINITELY HIDING SOMETHING.
*A.R.M. - ADVANCED ROBOT MACHINERY
WHY? HOW SO? CLARIFY!
JUST GRADING EXAMS AND PAPERS. NOTHING NEW TO REPORT.
I'LL BE SURE TO STAY IN TOUCH!
I KNOW. WE'LL SEND IN AN AGENT TO FIND OUT WHAT.

DR. TRU IS TRIPPIN'. WE'RE READY.
HE DOESN'T EVEN HAVE POWERS. HOW WOULD HE KNOW?
I THINK HE'S JUST LOOKING OUT FOR US.
BEEP! BEEP! BEEP!
EMERGENCY
THINK WE ULD LOOK TO THIS.
BEEP! BEEP! BEEP!
OH MY GOD! THOSE PEOPLE, TH-THEY'RE GOING TO...
MYA, THEY'RE GOING TO BE SAFE! BECAUSE WE'RE GOING TO SAVE THEM!
NOW...
WHO'S WITH ME?
IF WE CAN MAKE A DIFFERENCE, I'M IN!
I WAS WAITING ON YOU TWO!
"HERE'S THE PLAN..."
"SAVE THE PEOPLE..."
...AND PUT THEM BACK BEFORE HE NOTICES!
"WE BORROW THE SUITS..."

POWERS ON FLEEK!
MINDSET.
K-SWAG.

TURN UP!
BLAZE.
WE ABOUT TO GET LIT!

MILESTONE ARTS DISTRICT...
WE ARE LIVE FROM THE DOWNTOWN ARTS DISTRICT WHERE WITNESSES SAY A MAN IN A GAS MASK SHOT FIRE FROM HIS HANDS...
...SETTING FIRE TO THE HP NETWORK TOWER! COULD THIS BE THE INFAMOUS SPARK FLY? THE META HUMAN...
...ALLEGEDLY RESPONSIBLE FOR THE OUTBREAK OF FIRES AROUND THE CITY?
THE KCPD IS AT THEIR WITS END DEALING WITH META HUMAN CRIMINALS. THIS IS TONYA DOSS REPORTING LIVE.
FIRE CHIEF! A WORD! I'M DETECTIVE TYSON.
THIS IS MY PARTNER, DETECTIVE MURDOCK. HOW'S IT LOOKING?
THERE ARE A FEW PEOPLE ON THE SECOND FLOOR...
BUT WITH THE WEAKENED STRUCTURE AND BLOCKED FIRE EXIT, WE WOULDN'T GET OUT IN TIME.
MAYBE WE CAN HELP!

WHAT THE-- WHO ARE YOU?
WE'RE... UH... WE'RE SWAG PATROL
HALLOWEEN IS OVER, KID! THIS IS A RESTRICTED AREA!
SOMEONE ESCORT THEM OUTTA HERE.
WAIT! WE HAVE SPECIAL ABILITIES.
WE'RE METAS!
OKAY KIDS. IF YOU REALLY THINK YOU CAN HELP--
SIR, I KNOW WE CAN!
OKAY THEN. LET'S SEE WHAT YOU'VE GOT!
IF YOU'VE BEEN WATCHING THE NEWS, YOU'LL KNOW WE THINK THIS IS SPARK FLY'S DOING.
I-I THINK I SEE HIM. DON'T WORRY, WE GOT YOU.
BLAZE, MINDSET, GO RESCUE THE PEOPLE STILL TRAPPED INSIDE.
I'LL TAKE CARE OF SPARKY.
ARE YOU SURE YOU CAN TAKE HIM BY YOUR-SELF?
META OR NOT, HE'S STILL AN ARSONIST AND THEY LOVE TO WATCH THEIR HANDY-WORK, SO THERE'S A GOOD CHANCE HE'S STILL NEARBY.
DOES KOBE HAVE FIVE RINGS? NOW LET'S MOVE!

BEAUTIFUL!
I'M TAKING YOU DOWN, SPARK FLY!
HMPH! THE POLICE MUST BE GETTING DESPERATE IF THEY'RE SENDING A BOY IN TO DO THEIR JOB.
THE NAME IS K-SWAG! WE'LL SEE WHO'S A BOY WHEN I'M DONE!
SKREECH!
YOU ABOUT TO TAKE THIS "L" LIKE MEEK MILL!
TISH! TISH! TISH!
HA HA HA! THAT TICKLES!
FRAP! FRAP! FRAP!
...BUT THIS WON'T!!
THWACK!
OKAY, I MUST ADMIT! I HADN'T BEEN IN A FIST FIGHT SINCE EIGHTH GRADE!
UGH!
EVEN WORSE, THAT PUNCH MADE ME FEEL LIKE MY BONES WERE ON FIRE!

YOU GOT LUCKY!
FWOOSH!
YOU DON'T GET IT DO YOU, K-SWAG?
FIRE FUELS ME! AND ABSORBING IT MAKES ME STRONGER!
SCHWOOM!
I COULD FEEL HIS PULL TUGGING AT MY VEINS; RIPPING THE HEAT AWAY FROM ME!
HEY... I HOPE YOU RESCUED THOSE PEOPLE, 'CAUSE I COULD REALLY USE YOUR HELP.
CLICK!
YES! YES! YES! OH HA HA! YES! CAN YOU FEEL IT! GENETIC FIRE! EACH WAVE OF HEAT RIPPLING BACK ON ITSELF!!
YOU WERE QUITE THE ENERGY SOURCE!
KRSSBDM!!

OKAY FLY FACE! YOU BETTER GET READY 'CAUSE SHAQ AND GASOL JUST CAME OFF THE BENCH!
BOOM!
I THOUGHT YOU COULD HANDLE HIM?
HE CAN ABSORB FIRE AND DISCHARGE IT! TOOK MY FLAME LIKE HE OWNED IT!
LET'S SEE IF WE CAN GIVE HIM A HEADACHE!
VVRRNN!
SYNAPTIC RELY IS NOTHING MORE THAN ELECTRICAL FIRE IN THE BRAIN! YOUR MENTAL ATTACKS ARE JUST MORE FOOD FOR MY CONSUMPTION
OKAY! THIS GUY IS GOING BEAST MODE BUT I'VE GOT AN IDEA!
FOOSH!
FOOSH!
REMEMBER WHAT DR. TRE SAID IN CLASS ABOUT FIRE NEEDING OXYGEN?
OH, YEAH!
I'LL SPEED AROUND HIM AND CUT OFF HIS OXYGEN.
THEN YOU HIT HIM WITH A FORCE FIELD, MINDSET!
GOT IT!

HOLD YOUR BREATH!
HUH!?!
PHOOSH!
PHOOSH!
PHOOSH!
PHOOSH!
ANY DAY NOW, MINDSET!
OKAY... NOW!
DO YOUR THING BLAZE!
I-I C-CAN'T BREATHE!
VWRRNN!
AIGHT, LET'S GET IT!
OH, YOU'RE GOING TO WISH YOU HAD THIS ON CAMERA! WORLDSTAR!!!
KRA
KRAKK!
ARRGH!

MOMENTS LATER...
Rescue
KEEP BAC
YO! DETECTIVE!
WE'VE GOT SOMETHING FOR YOU!
WE EVEN WRAPPED IT UP IN A BOW FOR YA!
SO PLEASE TELL THE PEOPLE IT'S SAFE NOW.
I LEARNED A LOT THAT DAY! "TEAMWORK MAKES THE DREAM WORK!" SAID & DONE!
INCREDIBLE! YOU ACTUALLY CAUGHT HIM! KCPD COULD GET USE TO HAVING YOU THREE AROUND!
THERE THEY ARE!

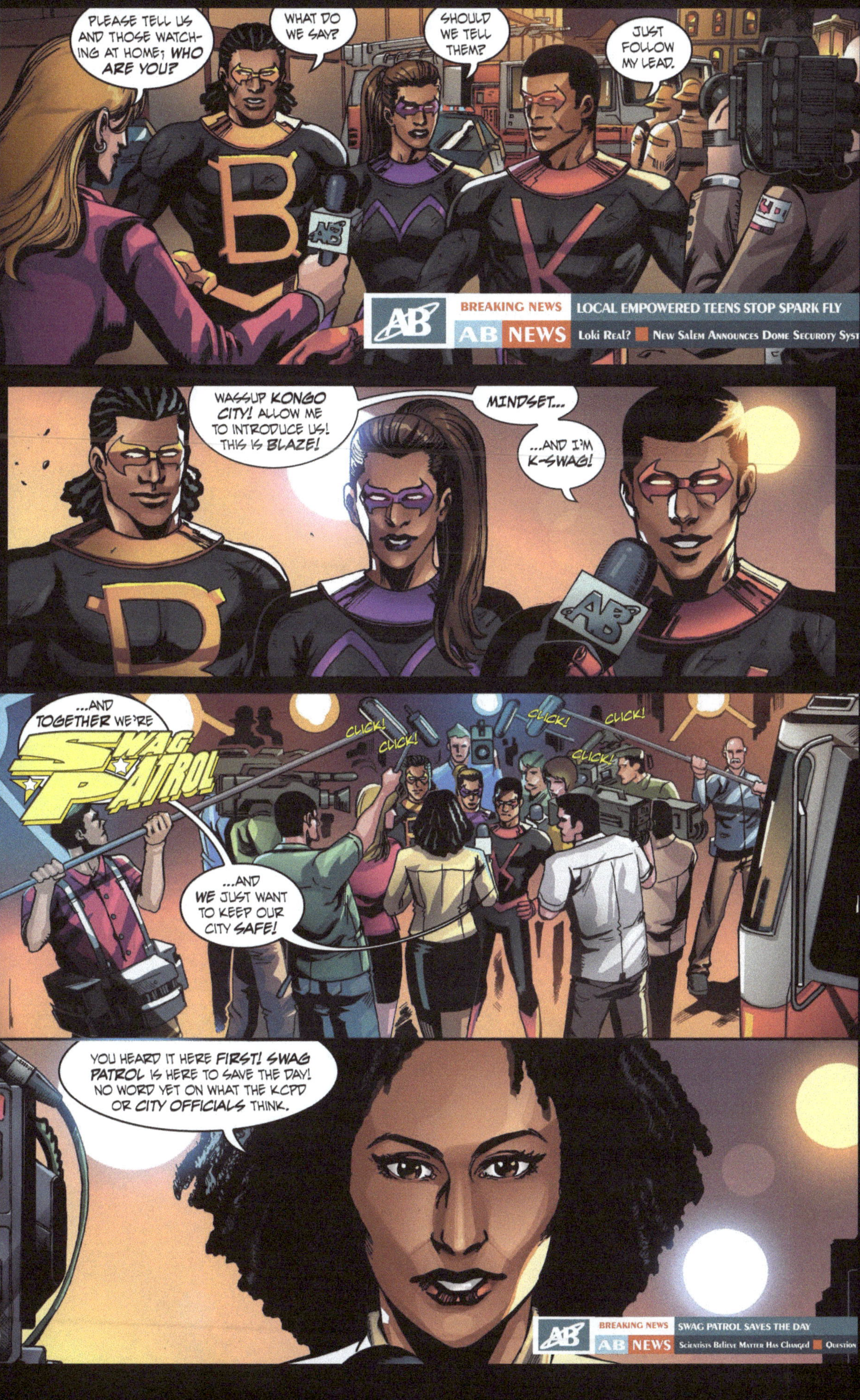

PLEASE TELL US AND THOSE WATCHING AT HOME; WHO ARE YOU?
WHAT DO WE SAY?
SHOULD WE TELL THEM?
JUST FOLLOW MY LEAD.
BREAKING NEWS
AB NEWS
LOCAL EMPOWERED TEENS STOP SPARK FLY
Loki Real?
New Salem Announces Dome Securoty Syst
WASSUP KONGO CITY! ALLOW ME TO INTRODUCE US! THIS IS BLAZE!
MINDSET...
...AND I'M K-SWAG!
...AND TOGETHER WE'RE SWAG PATROL
CLICK!
CLICK!
CLICK!
CLICK!
CLICK!
...AND WE JUST WANT TO KEEP OUR CITY SAFE!
YOU HEARD IT HERE FIRST! SWAG PATROL IS HERE TO SAVE THE DAY! NO WORD YET ON WHAT THE KCPD OR CITY OFFICIALS THINK.
BREAKING NEWS
AB NEWS
SWAG PATROL SAVES THE DAY
Scientists Believe Matter Has Changed
Question

ELSEWHERE...
I CAN'T LET A.R.M. FIND OUT ABOUT SWAG PATROL.
IT'S TOO DANGEROUS.
SINCE I GOT THEM INTO THIS MESS...
IT'S MY JOB TO KEEP THEM SAFE AND OUT OF HARM'S WAY.
SO WHO'S THE LEADER?
THAT WOULD BE YOUR'S TRULY!
<SIGH> TRE, WHAT HAVE YOU GOTTEN YOURSELF INTO?

ELSEWHERE...
BUZZ! BUZZ!
NEWS LIVE
YES, I'M WATCHING NOW...
THAT'S THEM...
WHAT'S THE POINT OF PAYING YOU THEN?
WE WILL, EVENTUALLY, BUT FIRST...
...LET'S SEE WHAT WE'RE UP AGAINST!

WHOOP! WHOOP!
TYSON, WHAT'S YOUR STATUS?
GLAD YOU ARRIVED, CAPTAIN HART! THOSE KIDS... THEY'RE SUPERHEROES! THEY CALL THEMSELVES SWAG PATROL!
SUPER HEROES?
I SEE, DETECTIVE. HERE'S WHAT I WANT YOU TO DO...
YES! THEY TOOK DOWN SPARK FLY IN MINUTES! WE'VE BEEN TRYING TO CATCH HIM FOR MONTHS!
WHAT!?
!?!
ARREST THEM!
TO BE CONTINUED...

CHAPTER 2

"IF YOU WANT TO GO QUICKLY, GO ALONE.

IF YOU WANT TO GO FAR, GO TOGETHER."

~ AFRICAN PROVERB

DID YOU HEAR ME, DETECTIVE? I SAID ARREST THEM!
BUT SIR—
THAT'S AN ORDER!
ANY IDEAS GETTING OUT OF THIS, FEARLESS LEADER?
THINKING!
EXECUTE THE ESCAPE PLAN FROM TRAINING!
DR. TRE?
GLAD TO KNOW THE COMMS WORK. GET OUT OF THERE AND GET BACK TO THE LAB IMMEDIATELY!
GOT IT! LET'S ROLL GUYS!

NO FLEXX ZONE
WRITTEN BY RUBYN WARREN AND GABE SMITH -- ART BY MARK MARVIDA
COLORS BY MARVIN MARVIDA -- LETTERS BY MICAH MYERS
COVER BY JEFFERY "CHAMBA" CRUZ
SORRY, OFFICERS, BUT WE GOTTA RUN!
THEY'RE ESCAPING!
Barber Shop
POLICE

BYE FELECIA!
IT'S PAST OUR CURFEW!
RESCUE

AND THEN YOU YELLED WORLDSTAR! THAT WAS CRAZY! JOB WELL DONE TEAM!
THESE VILLAINS AIN'T READY FOR US!
DO YOU THINK DR. TRE WILL BE MAD?
NAH I DON'T SEE WHY. WE KILLED IT TONIGHT!

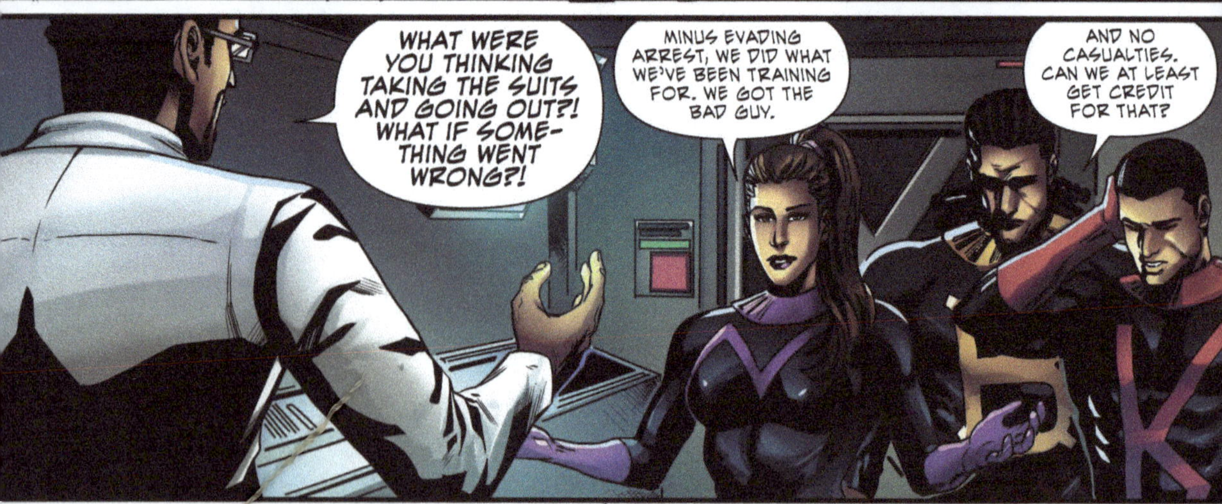

WHAT WERE YOU THINKING TAKING THE SUITS AND GOING OUT?! WHAT IF SOMETHING WENT WRONG?!
MINUS EVADING ARREST, WE DID WHAT WE'VE BEEN TRAINING FOR. WE GOT THE BAD GUY.
AND NO CASUALTIES. CAN WE AT LEAST GET CREDIT FOR THAT?

OH BOY...
WHAT HAVE I DONE! I NEED TO TELL THEM ABOUT A.R.M.*
*A.R.M. - ADVANCED ROBOT MACHINERY

I'M JUST CONCERNED FOR YOUR SAFETY. LEAVE YOUR UNIFORMS HERE AND I'LL SEE YOU TOMORROW. I AM PROUD OF YOU GUYS.

UH-OH!
6 Missed Calls
MOM

CARTER RESIDENCE.
I'M ONLY GONNA ASK Y'ALL ONE TIME! WHERE WERE YOU?
UM, SEE WHAT HAPPENED—
WE WERE AT THE SUPERHERO SIGHTING.
YEAH WE WERE ON THE WAY HOME WHEN IT HAPPENED SO WE STAYED AND WATCHED. SORRY WE DIDN'T CALL. IT WON'T HAPPEN AGAIN!
IT BETTER NOT OR THAT'S YOUR BEHIND! GO TO BED.
THAT WAS CLOSE!
NICE SAVE, BRUH! I OWE YOU!
WE WERE THERE, TECHNICALLY.

HAROLD'S CANDY.
ONE YEAR AGO.
ADD A LITTLE OF THIS TO THE TAFFY MIX AND WE ARE GOOD TO GO.
RICK FLETCHER!
MR. BLOOM, WHAT A SURPRISE.
YOU DIM-WITTED IMBECILE! HOW LONG DID YOU THINK I WOULDN'T NOTICE THAT YOU'VE BEEN STEALING COMPANY PROPERTY!?
SIR, PLEASE HEAR ME OUT... WHAT IF WE COULD APPLY THE CHEMICAL PROPERTIES OF TAFFY TO THE HUMAN BODY? OUR BODIES WOULD BE MORE DURABLE AND LESS PRONE TO INJURY. THAT'S WHAT I'VE BEEN USING MATERIALS FOR.
WE HIRED YOU TO CREATE FORMULAS FOR OUR ASSORTED CANDIES, NOT SO YOU COULD PLAY MAD SCIENTIST!
BUT THIS COULD BE A HUGE DISCOVERY FOR MODERN MEDICINE! I'VE MADE A SAMPLE OF THE TAFFY THAT I BELIEVE TO BE ALMOST READY FOR HUMAN TRIALS, ALL I NEED--
I CERTAINLY WOULDN'T WANT TO WORK WITH A LOW LIFE THIEF! YOU'RE FIRED! AND YOU'RE LUCKY I DON'T CALL THE AUTHORITIES. ESCORT THIS LYING CRACKPOT OFF THE PREMISES!
HOW DARE YOU EMBARRASS ME LIKE THIS!? AFTER ALL I'VE DONE FOR THIS COMPANY?! YOU'LL REGRET THIS, BLOOM!
GOOD RIDDANCE!

DANIEL HALE WILLIAMS HIGH SCHOOL.
PRESENT DAY.
RIIIIIINNNGGG
Daniel Hale Williams High School
WASSUP, RASHAD AND CHRIS!
LAWRENCE! WHAT'S GOOD, SERGIO?
I'M GOOD, PLAYA! I SEE YOU PUTTING THE MOVES ON DENISE!
NAH. WE JUST FRIENDS.
RIIIGHT!
DID YOU GUYS WATCH THE NEWS LAST NIGHT?
NO WHAT'S GOING ON?
HOW DID YOU NOT HEAR ABOUT THOSE SUPER GUYS? IT WAS EVERYWHERE. REALMENTE LOCO* YO!
*REALLY CRAZY.
OH YEAH, THE SWAG GUYS.
I SAW SOMETHING ABOUT IT ON IG.
HERE GOES ACTUAL FOOTAGE SOMEONE RECORDED. OVER 1,000,000 VIEWS SINCE LAST NIGHT.
WHAT DO THE COMMENTS SAY?
SwagPatrol
RunFlashRun 5 hours ago
The red dude is dope AF!
Reply
Wakanda4Ever 3 hours ago
#teamSwagPatrol
Reply
HarlyKwinLvr 1 hour ago
The orange one is my favorite!
Reply

YO DID YOU SEE THE FLYING CHICK IN THE PURPLE?
MAN SHE WAS THICK!
YEAH SHE BAD!
HEY, CUTIE! LET ME TALK TO YOU REAL QUICK!
GIRL YOU MUST BE TIRED 'CAUSE YOU'VE BEEN RUNNING THROUGH MY MIND ALL DAY!
JUST GREAT!
HEY I'M--
YOU OK, GIRL?
I'M FINE, CANDACE.
I KNOW YOU SAW THE NEWS LAST NIGHT?
OH YEAH, THE SUPER TEENS RIGHT?
YES, THE ONE IN THE RED IS SOOO FINE!

EWWW! HE IS NOT ALL THAT!
WHATEVER, THAT'S BAE!

MEANWHILE.
Police Station "EST. 1949"
SIR, PLEASE RECONSIDER!
YOU'LL BE MAKING A HUGE MISTAKE DOING THIS!
I HAVE A CITY TO THINK ABOUT, TYSON. IT'S FULL OF FREAKS ALREADY AND I WON'T ADD SUPERPOWERED DELINQUENTS TO THE LIST! THEY'RE JUST KIDS!
CAPT. HART
I'VE SEEN FIRST HAND WHAT THOSE KIDS CAN DO. THEY'D PROBABLY DO A BETTER JOB THAN YOU IF YOU LET 'EM!
I WANT YOU TO CHOOSE YOUR NEXT FEW WORDS CAREFULLY BEFORE WE HAVE ONE LESS DETECTIVE AROUND HERE.
CAPTAIN, THEY'RE READY FOR YOU.
KNOCK! KNOCK!
COME IN!

I'M SURE YOU ALL KNOW BY NOW THAT KONGO CITY WAS VISITED LAST NIGHT BY THREE YOUNG PEOPLE WHO HAVE DECIDED TO TAKE THE LAW INTO THEIR OWN HANDS. THIS HAS RAISED CONCERNS FOR MANY CITIZENS.
AS A PRECAUTION TO PREVENT EXPENSIVE DAMAGES AND ENSURE THE SAFETY OF EVERYONE, THE GROUP CALLING THEMSELVES SWAG PATROL, ARE TO STAY AWAY FROM ANY AND ALL POLICE MATTERS.
THIS IS GRADE A BULL@%^$!
VIGILANTISM WILL NOT BE TOLERATED IN KONGO CITY!
HMM. DET. TYSON DOESN'T SEEM TOO THRILLED ABOUT THIS.
THAT IS ALL. THANK YOU FOR YOUR TIME.
CAN SWAG PATROL BE TRUSTED?
IS SWAG PATROL ANTI-POLICE?

I CAN'T BELIEVE HE WOULD MAKE A CALL LIKE THAT! DOESN'T HE SEE HOW VALUABLE THEY COULD BE TO US!? TO THE CITY!?
ZWOOM
WHAT THE--?
For when you need to reach us. -SP
WILL DO, FRIENDS!

SIX MONTHS AGO.

THIS IS IT! I'VE SPENT THE LAST OF MY SAVINGS ON THIS BATCH OF TAFFY. I'LL PROVE THAT IDIOT BLOOM AND EVERYONE ELSE WHO DOUBTED ME WRONG!

COMMENCING HUMAN TRIAL NUMBER ONE... NO IMMEDIATE EFFECTS SO FAR...OTHER THAN THE BITTER TASTE I DON'T FEEL ANY--

AGGHHH! NOW FEELING...INTENSE PAIN...SUBJECT EXPERIENCING...

AGH!

REC 30m28s

PRESENT DAY.
EVENING AT HAROLD'S CANDY FACTORY.
THESE THIRD QUARTER SALES ARE ATROCIOUS! IF THESE NUMBERS DON'T CHANGE, I GUARANTEE ALL OF YOU BUMS WILL BE DRAGGED TO THE UNEMPLOYMENT LINE LIKE FLETCHER!
HONK! HONK! HONK!
FIRE
MR. BLOOM, THERE IS A DISTURBANCE ON THE FIRST FLOOR! THE POLICE ARE ON THEIR WAY.
MAKE SURE IT GETS HANDLED, I'M IN A MEETING.
MR. BLOOM! WHATEVER WAS ON THE FIRST FLOOR IS NOW UP HERE COMING F--
BOW.
NNN-NNO. IT CAN'T BE! RICK?!

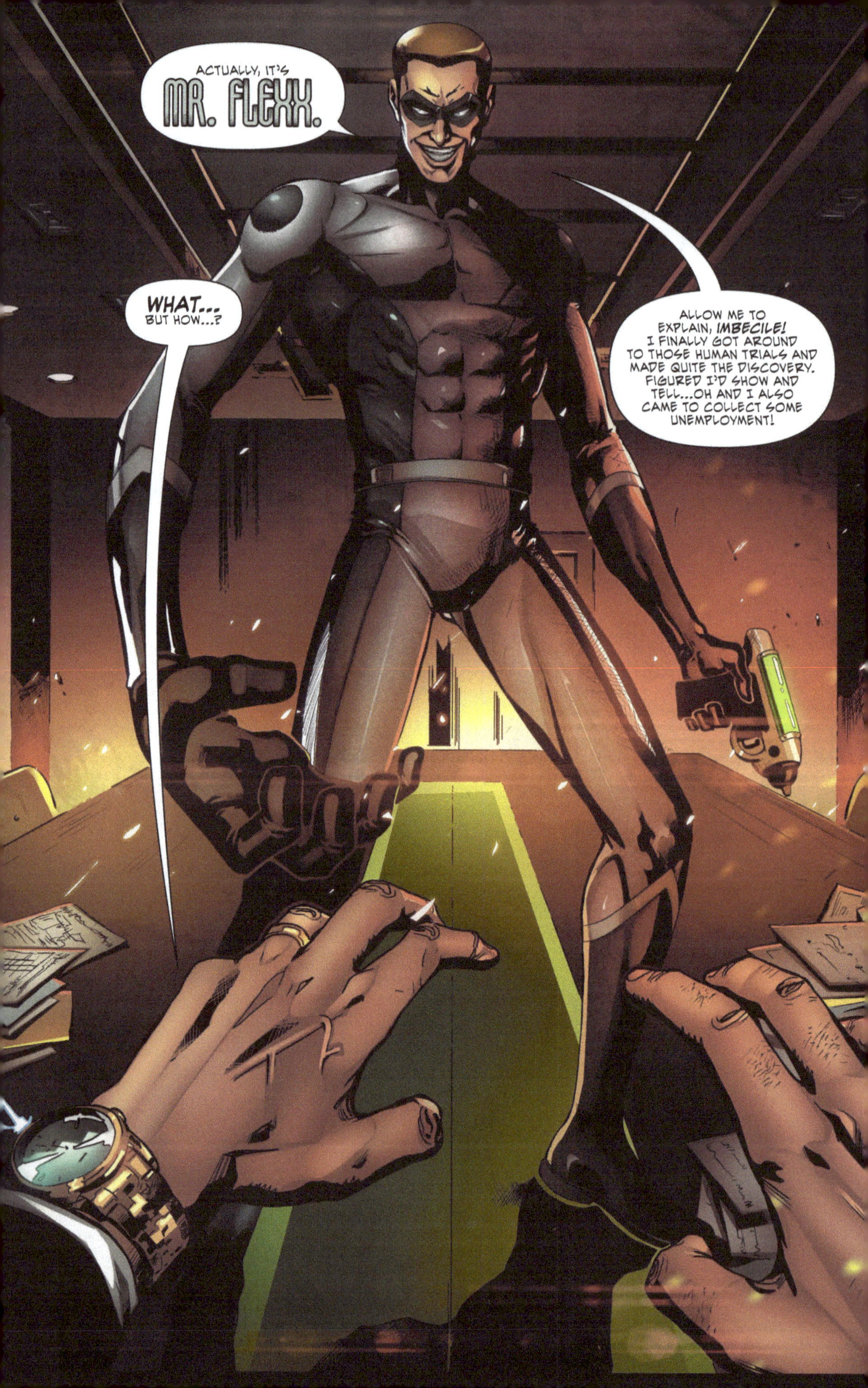

ACTUALLY, IT'S MR. FLEXX.
WHAT... BUT HOW...?
ALLOW ME TO EXPLAIN, IMBECILE! I FINALLY GOT AROUND TO THOSE HUMAN TRIALS AND MADE QUITE THE DISCOVERY. FIGURED I'D SHOW AND TELL...OH AND I ALSO CAME TO COLLECT SOME UNEMPLOYMENT!

WE ALMOST AT TWO MILLION VIEWS!
I DON'T THINK WE SHOULD BE CELEBRATING AFTER ONE FIGHT. LET'S FOCUS ON IMPROVEMENT. FOR ALL WE KNOW, WE GOT LUCKY LAST NIGHT.
OUR FIRST VID JUST WENT VIRAL!
IT'S NOT LUCK, DOC, WE JUST GOT IT LIKE THAT!
NEXT VID PUT A VILLAIN IN A SPIRAL!

BEEP! BEEP!
DETECTIVE TYSON
SWAG PATROL, DO YOU COPY?

LOUD AND CLEAR, DETECTIVE. WHAT'S THE PROBLEM?

WE HAVE A SITUATION AT HAROLD'S CANDY. A META HUMAN CALLING HIMSELF, MR. FLEXX HAS ENTERED THE BUILDING TAKING EVERYONE HOSTAGE.
GOT IT! ON OUR WAY!

NOT TO SOUND LIKE AN OVERPROTECTIVE PARENT BUT PLEASE BE CAREFUL OUT THERE. OTHER THAN DETECTIVE TYSON, THE POLICE AREN'T ON OUR SIDE. PROCEED WITH CAUTION.
APPRECIATE THE CONCERN BUT WE GOT THIS! LET'S SUIT UP!

AFTER YOU GIVE ME EVERYTHING IN YOUR POCKETS, YOU WILL TAKE ME TO THE SAFE.
AND THEN YOU'LL LET US GO RIGHT?
THEY WILL BE FREE TO LEAVE, BUT I'M NOT SURE ABOUT YOU.
STOP RIGHT THERE, MR. FLEXX!
YOU GOIN' DOWN!
AND YOU ARE?
DON'T YOU WATCH TV?
OR YOUTUBE?
WE'RE SWAG PATROL!
WHOEVER YOU ARE, THIS MATTER DOESN'T CONCERN YOU BRATS!
SAME ROUTINE LIKE BEFORE?
YEP.

DUMB STRETCHY DUDE SAY WHAT?
WHAT?
ZWOOSH!
COMIN AT YA' RUBBER BAND BRAIN!
DIDN'T THEY TEACH YOU IN SCHOOL...
NOT TO RUN IN THE HALL?
BOING!
WHOA!
UGGH...
LOW KEY, THIS WOULD BE A FUN RIDE!
GOTTA WORK OUT THE LANDING THOUGH!

GET READY TO CATCH THIS FADE, FAM!
YOU KIDS ARE SO PREDICTABLE!
WHOA!
MY TURN!
I WAS HONESTLY EXPECTING A CHALLENGE FROM YOU GUYS!
OOMF!
THUD!!
HOW DO MORE GUYS NOTICE ME WITH MY MASK ON? YOU CAN'T EVEN SEE MY FACE GOOD.
EARTH TO MINDSET! WE NEED A FORCE FIELD AROUND THIS DUDE!
RIGHT. ON IT!

COME ON! STAY IN PLACE!
AM I NOT CUTE ENOUGH? MAYBE I SHOULD CHANGE MY HAIR OR SOMETHING TO GET THEM TO NOTICE ME.
FOR SOME REASON I CAN'T SUSTAIN A FORCE FIELD. I DON'T KNOW WHAT'S GOING ON WITH MY POWER!
NEVER MIND THEN! MINDSET IS M.I.A SO I'M GONNA DISTRACT HIM, THAT'S WHEN YOU HIT HIM WITH A BLAST.
COOL!
DEE WHO?
I GOTTA GIVE IT TO YOU, RUBBER BAND. YOU PUT UP A GOOD FIGHT. DO YOU KNOW DEE?
AHH!
DEEZ NUTS!
SHRACKWOOM!

INTERESTING, THE SUBJECTS SEEM TO HAVE BOUNCED BACK FROM THE GIRL'S MISHAP.
IT APPEARS THE SUBJECTS HAVE NOW GAINED THE UPPER HAND IN COMBAT.
HE'S GONNA LOVE WATCHING THIS!

IMPRESSIVE TRICK...
BUT LETS CALL IT A NIGHT SHALL WE?
CRASH!
FOLLOW ME, SWAG PATROL AND SHE DIES!
AAAAHHHHH!
NEXT ISSUE: ALL FALLS DOWN

CHAPTER 3

"If relatives help each other,

what evil can hurt them?"

~ African proverb

LATE NIGHT. THE HOME OF LUCIUS JACKSON.
IS THIS SEAT TAKEN?
I'M ACTUALLY SAVING IT FOR A FRIEND.
ALWAYS ONE FOR JOKES, LUCIUS.
TELL ME, FELECIA, WHAT'S YOUR EVALUATION?

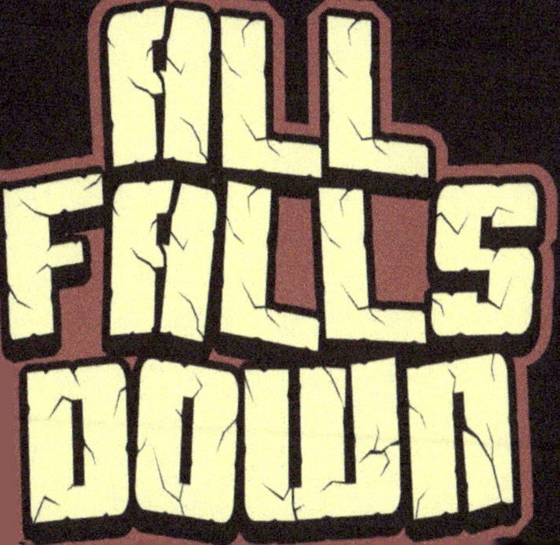

Written by
RUBYN WARREN & GABE SMITH
Art by
MARK MARVIDA
Colors by
MARVIN MARVIDA
Letters by
BRANT FOWLER
Cover by
JEFFERY "CHAMBA" CRUZ

AN HOUR AGO.
WHAT HAPPENED?
HE... HE GOT AWAY.
DO WE GO AFTER HIM?
NO, COME BACK TO BASE AND LET THE AUTHORITIES HANDLE IT. YOU GUYS DID GOOD.
WHAT ARE YOU STANDING THERE FOR? GO GET THAT LUNATIC!
SORRY BUT WE HAVE TO GO.
THAT'S IT?! WHAT KIND OF HEROES ARE YOU?!
WE SAVED YOUR STUCK UP--
LET'S HEAD BACK TO BASE.
FREEZE!

I DIDN'T ASK YOU ANYTHING! IF YOU MAKE ANY SUDDEN MOVE--
OFFICER, THE CRIMINAL GOT AWAY. THEY TRIED TO STOP HIM.
YOU KNOW WE'RE THE GOOD GUYS, RIGHT?
MINDSET...
I ALREADY HAVE A FORCE FIELD ON DECK.
LOWER YOUR WEAPONS NOW!
ARE YOU CRAZY?! YOU'RE GONNA SHOOT THREE, BLACK, META TEENS ATTEMPTING TO HELP?! DO YOU WANT A SITUATION WORSE THAN FERGUSON ON OUR HANDS?!
SORRY, SIR--
I WILL DEAL WITH YOU TOMORROW!
YOU GUYS CAN'T BE HERE!
NO DISRESPECT, BUT WE HAVE AN OBLIGATION TO DO THIS!
WELL YOUR OBLIGATION CAUSED A CRIMINAL TO ESCAPE WITH A HOSTAGE. I'M TELLING YOU STAY AWAY! NEXT TIME I WILL BRING YOU GUYS IN. NOW GET OUTTA HERE!

THE POLICE ALMOST MADE US A HASHTAG TONIGHT!
THAT WAS MORE FRIGHTENING THAN SPARK FLY AND MR. FLEXX COMBINED! EVEN AS A SUPERHERO--
THEY STILL ONLY SEE BLACK!
SOME GOOD NEWS, I CHECKED POLICE SCANNERS AND THE HOSTAGE WAS FOUND SAFE A FEW BLOCKS AWAY. MR. FLEXX JUST USED HER TO ESCAPE BUT HE'S STILL AT LARGE.
I BLASTED HIM SO IT'S NOT MY FAULT.
APPARENTLY YOU DIDN'T BLAST HIM HARD ENOUGH. HE GOT AWAY!
I KNOW YOU AIN'T TALKING! HE HAD YOU FLYING BACK LIKE A SLINGSHOT!
IT'S REALLY MYA'S FAULT!
NO IT'S NOT!
THEN PLEASE EXPLAIN WHAT HAPPENED TO YOU TONIGHT!
I DON'T KNOW! FOR SOME REASON MY POWERS JUST WENT OUT.
MAYBE IF YOU WASN'T BEING SLOW IN LA LA LAND YOU WOULD'VE GOT HIM WHEN I TOLD YOU!
IT WASN'T...

MY FAULT!
YOU REALLY GOTTA LEARN HOW TO SHUT UP SOMETIMES.
LESSON LEARNED. TRUST ME!
RASHAD! I'M SO SORRY! I DIDN'T MEAN TO... I GOTTA GO!

TONIGHT, ESPECIALLY AFTER WHAT JUST TRANSPIRED, HAS SHOWN THAT WE HAVE A LOT MORE WORK TO DO.
WE'LL GET IT RIGHT NEXT TIME.
THERE WON'T BE A NEXT TIME FOR NOW. THE SUITS ARE GOING BACK IN THE CASE.
WHAT?!
YOU CAN'T JUST END THE TEAM!
WE JUST GOT STARTED AND NOW YOU PUTTING US ON THE BENCH?!
THIS IS NOT UP FOR DISCUSSION!
BUT--
UNTIL YOU GUYS CAN SHOW ME THAT WE'RE READY FOR THIS, SWAG PATROL IS OUT OF COMMISSION. UNDERSTOOD?
YES, SIR.
THIS SOME BULL--
LANGUAGE, CHRIS! NOW I'LL GO TALK TO MYA.

MYA, HOW ARE YOU FEELING?
I ALSO WANT YOU TO COME BACK TO THE LAB TOMORROW SO WE CAN RUN TEST ON YOU.
SOUNDS GOOD.
DON'T WORRY, MYA, YOU'RE ONE OF MY BRIGHTEST STUDENTS, I KNOW YOU'LL COME OUT OF THIS SHINING!

HOW WOULD YOU FEEL IF YOU TOSSED YOUR BROTHER ACROSS THE ROOM? WHAT HAPPENED TO ME IN THERE?

I BELIEVE YOU DEVELOPED TELEKINESIS, THE ABILITY TO MOVE OBJECTS WITH YOUR MIND.
GREAT, ANOTHER UN-CONTROLLABLE ABILITY TO ADD TO MY LIST. SORRY ABOUT THAT.
RASHAD WILL BE OK BUT THE TEAM IS GOING ON HIATUS FOR A WHILE UNTIL WE GET BETTER.
KINDA FIGURED THAT.

THANKS, DR. TRE!

AFTER SCHOOL THE NEXT DAY.
Daniel Hale Williams High School

IT'S THAT EASY?
I GUESS RASHAD HAS ALL THE ANSWERS!

I'M JUST SAYING, THE KEY TO THESE GIRLS IS JUST SHOOT YOUR SHOT. GET OUT OF YOUR HEAD AND JUST TALK TO 'EM.

WHAT'S UP, DENISE?
HEY, RASHAD.

YOU'VE LIKED HER FOR THE LONGEST! HOW ABOUT YOU SHOW US WHAT YOU TALKING ABOUT!
YEAH, GO SHOOT YOUR SHOT, PAPI!

OH... OK. TAKE NOTES.

YO, DENISE!
I SEE YOU OUT HERE LOOKING GOOD, TRYNA SHOW A BROTHA WHAT YOU WORKING WITH AND I ACCEPT.
ACCEPT WHAT?
YOU AND ME GOING OUT THIS WEEKEND. YOU AIN'T GOTTA HIDE NO MORE.
BOY BYE! YOU CUTE BUT IMMA NEED YOU TO COME CORRECT. I'M NOT ONE OF YOUR BASKETBALL GROUPIES. IT'S A NO!
BUT--
MAYBE SOME OTHER TIME.
THAT'S HOW IT'S SUPPOSED TO GO?!
AT LEAST YOU SHOT YOUR SHOT!
STEPH CURRY DOESN'T MAKE EVERY THREE!
DAWG, YOU JUST MISSED A FREE THROW!
MORE LIKE AN EASY LAY UP!

DHW FOOTBALL FIELD.

WHY ME? IT SEEMS LIKE EVERYTHING I LOVE IS TAKEN AWAY FROM ME. FIRST MY PARENTS LEAVE ME TO PLAY DOCTOR FOR THE WORLD.

THEN GRANDMA, THE WOMAN THAT HELPED RAISED ME, DIES A COUPLE YEARS AGO. THEN ME AND MY COUSINS BECOME SUPERHEROES WITH OUR OWN TEAM!

NOW THAT'S GONE! ALL I SEEM TO DO IS LOSE!

AGGGHHH!

HEY, AUNTIE... CAN YOU COME GET ME?

CHRIS, I'VE TOLD YOU ALREADY ABOUT THE UNNECESSARY ROUGHNESS! HIT THE SHOWERS FOR TODAY! YOU'RE DONE!

THINKING ABOUT GRANDMA?
THAT AND THEN SOME!
I MISS HER TOO!
WHEN ME AND THE KIDS LOST ROBERT, IT WAS HARD AT FIRST BUT EVERY DAY GETS A LITTLE BETTER. I KNOW IT'S BEEN A LOT FOR YOU WITH YOUR PARENTS TRAVELING, GRANDMA GONE AND ADJUSTING WITH US NOW SO IF YOU EVER WANNA TALK PLEASE DO. DON'T KEEP IT BOTTLED UP.
IT JUST FEELS LIKE WHEN IT STARTS TO GO GOOD FOR ME, LIFE DECIDES TO TAKE ME FOR A LOOP. BUT I AM THANKFUL THAT YOU TOOK ME IN.
THAT'S LIFE BUT YOU HAVE TO KEEP MOVING FORWARD IN THE RIGHT DIRECTION. AND DON'T FEEL LIKE YOU'RE A CHARITY CASE. WE LOVE HAVING YOU AROUND! YOU'RE FAMILY AND FAMILY ALWAYS LOOKS OUT FOR EACH OTHER! REMEMBER THAT.
I'LL NEVER FORGET IT, AUNTIE!

TODAY WE'RE GONNA RUN A FEW EXERCISES AND THEN TEST YOUR NEWEST ABILITY.
IF I CAN GET IT TO WORK...

YOUR LEVELS SEEM NORMAL. NOTHING OUT OF THE ORDINARY.
NOW I WANT YOU TO USE YOUR TELEKINESIS TO MOVE THE APPLE.
DR. TRE, I DON'T KNOW HOW TO DO THIS.
JUST TRY TO FOCUS.
MYA, YOU'RE DOING IT!

IT'S REALLY WORKING!
YOUR NEUROLOGICAL LEVELS ARE OFF THE CHARTS! INCREDIBLE!
WITH THIS NEW ABILITY AND READINGS, SHE IS DEFINITELY THE MOST POWERFUL OF THEM. HER POTENTIAL IS UNLIMITED.
WHAT DID YOU SAY?
I SAID INCREDIBLE!
AND YOU SAID SOMETHING AFTER THAT.
NO, THAT WAS THE LAST THING I SAID.

MYA, WHAT HAPPENED?
I FORGOT... I HAVE A BIG PAPER DUE TOMORROW. I HAVE TO GO.
OK. WE MADE GREAT PROGRESS TODAY! I'LL SEE YOU LATER.
YEP. SEE YOU LATER, DOC.
NO... I CAN'T... CAN I?... DID I READ HIS MIND?!

I THINK SHUTTING THEM DOWN FOR A WHILE WILL KEEP THEM OFF A.R.M.'S RADAR FOR NOW...
Detective Tyson
BEEP BEEP BEEP
THIS RABBIT HOLE GETS DEEPER EVERY DAY!
Det. Tyson: We need to meet tonight.

JACKSON CONSOLIDATED, INC.

AND NOW I'D LIKE TO INTRODUCE TO YOU OUR LATEST PROJECT IN DEVELOPMENT.

MEET THE TERRA GLOVES. WITH THESE ON, THE USER WOULD BE ABLE TO CONTROL ROCK MATTER WITH EASE.

IT'S STILL IN THE EARLY STAGES OF PRODUCTION BUT THESE HAVE THE POTENTIAL TO REVOLUTIONIZE THE CONSTRUCTION AND ARCHITECT INDUSTRY. TERRA GLOVES ARE THE FUTURE!

LUCIUS, THAT'S SOME INVENTION! I CAN'T WAIT TO SEE THE PROTOTYPE.
THAT WILL BE HERE SOONER THAN YOU THINK.
LUCIUS...

...WE NEED TO TALK.

I MAY HAVE THE ANSWER TO YOUR DILEMMA.
EXCELLENT!

IT WASN'T EASY. I WENT THROUGH QUITE A FEW CONTACTS...
...BUT I FINALLY GOT IN TOUCH WITH TWO INDIVIDUALS...
ARE YOU SURE?
...WHO CAN GET THE JOB DONE.
YES. THEY CAME HIGHLY RECOMMENDED. THEY'RE A LITTLE OVER THE TOP BUT BASED ON THEIR TRACK RECORD, I'M SURE THEY'LL DELIVER.
LUCIUS, I WANT YOU TO MEET...

LAUGH NOW AND CRY LATER.

ENJOYED WHAT YOU READ?
LET US KNOW ONLINE!
@SWAGPATROLCOMIC
SWAG PATROL
NEXT ISSUE: HOLLYWOOD SHUFFLE, PART 1

LETTER PATROL

Thanks for reading this exciting volume of Swag Patrol! This is our letters column where you, the fans, can tell us your thoughts, predictions and more about the series and I respond. Let's get into it!

Hello, Mr. Warren,

My name is Jermaine, and I just wanted to contact you and tell you that I've pretty much been your fan for a little while now, ever since I first happened upon your "0-Issue" Swag Patrol origins.

Everything about it just clicked with me. It hit so many of the cool and classic superhero beats that I love and doing so featuring an all-Black cast of heroes (that warms the child-me who would have love to have had this in the 90's growing up), while also having a pleasantly surprising amount of depth, particularly with Rashad (that 16 year-old kid's got to work on that classroom diligence that doesn't lead to getting told off by his teachers and getting his stuff confiscated if he wants to carry out his otherwise impressively planned out career path into the Criminal Justice field) and the almost infamous Dr. Tre (conspiracy theory time, but I have the sneaking feeling the good Dr.'s not being as forthcoming with all of his motives and goals. I believe his heart is ultimately good and righteous, but there's a lot he's not telling the Swag Patrol, and other indicators, too, like for example how he had those chemicals practically just lying around in his classroom otherwise out in the open; if he didn't "Chessmaster" plan that accident, I get the feeling he had intended on eventually bestowing the right students, chosen from his careful observations as the otherwise innocuous high school science teacher, with these powers, and that's further backed up by how relatively quick he was to plant the hero idea into the kids' heads. And all that sweet equipment that he has. One way or the other, I get the feeling Dr. Tre planned this, and if not specifically with the trio he got, he certainly rolled with the proverbial punches).

Last but not least, and I know this is kinda early bird, but I wonder if the Swag Patrol will gain any new teen members, powered by science or other means? Especially if my above hunch on Dr. Tre is in anyway accurate, it be cool to see who, if any, would have been among his first choice(s) that might/could join later anyway.

Well, I've fan boyed you long enough. It was awesome getting a chance to leave this message to you. Your creation has come a long way, and I want it to go even further and further still!

Sincerely, your new-old Swag Patrol fanboy,

Jermaine

Hey Jermaine,

Thanks for your heart felt letter! I really appreciate coming across a true and sincere fan! As far as Dr. Tre goes, without giving away too much, there is more to Dr. Tre and we'll be delving into this a little more in the future so stay

tuned! Also, I can attest that Swag Patrol wasn't planned at all… that's all I'll say for now. And as far as new members joining the team, that's possible but definitely no time soon. I'm glad my characters and story resonate with you and I can't wait for you to see what we have in store for future issues.

Until next time,

Rubyn Warren

That's all the letters we have for now. If you enjoy the series, have questions, comments, concerns, fan art or fan theories email us and let us know. You may see it printed in the next issue! Thanks for all the support and see you in Issue 4.

Fan art by Don Edwards

Fan art by Tim Harris

BEHIND THE SCENES

I CAME UP WITH THE IDEA FOR SWAG PATROL 10 YEARS AGO WHILE I WAS STILL IN HIGH SCHOOL. I LOVED X-MEN, STATIC SHOCK AND SPIDERMAN GROWING UP SO I WANTED TO MAKE HEROES I THOUGHT WERE JUST AS COOL AS THEM! HERE ARE SOME OF MY ORIGINAL DRAWINGS.

ORIGINALLY I NAMED HIM K-SWAG AND THE K STOOD FOR KAPTAIN (CRINGEY, I KNOW). EVENTUALLY I DECIDED TO JUST NAME HIM K-SWAG WITHOUT KAPTAIN BECAUSE THE NAME SOUNDED COOL AND UNIQUE TO ME. RASHAD IS KINDA MY ALTER EGO (NOT REALLY) AND I ALWAYS THOUGHT SUPER SPEED AND FIRE WERE REALLY COOL ABILITIES SO THAT'S HOW I DECIDED HIS POWER SET.

MINDSET WAS INITIALLY CALLED G-SWAG AND THE G STOOD FOR GIRL (WHAT WAS I THINKING?!). AFTER I DECIDED ON HER PSYCHIC POWERS I FINALLY CAME UP WITH A NAME THAT REFLECTED THEM. MY CO WRITER GABE THOUGHT IT'D BE COOL TO GIVE HER NEW ABILITIES SO I'M EXCITED TO SEE WHERE WE GO WITH HER NOW!

I FIRST CALLED HIM B-SWAG AND THE B STOOD FOR BOY (I WAS 16, DON'T JUDGE ME LOL). I LOOSELY BASED HIM ON MY COUSIN WHO SPENT THE WHOLE SUMMER WITH US, HENCE WHY HE LIVES WITH HIS COUSINS. AT FIRST, I DIDN'T WANT TO GIVE HIM SUPER STRENGTH BECAUSE IT SEEMED GENERIC. THAT MADE ME THINK TO GIVE THEM MORE THAN ONE ABILITY. ALSO DON'T KNOW WHY I GAVE HIM ALL THE LINES BEHIND HIS B, THE SIMPLE FOUR LINES LOOK WAY BETTER!

I BASED DR. TRE OFF OF MY HIP HOP PRODUCTION TEACHER, MR. TRU. HE WAS ONE OF THE COOLEST TEACHERS I HAD AND HIS INSIGHT AND WANT TO HELP US BE BETTER IS WHAT DR. TRE IS ALL ABOUT WITH SWAG PATROL. I ALSO THOUGHT IT'D BE COOL AT 16 TO SEE A BLACK MAN BE SMART AND INTO SCIENCE BUT HAVE SOME SUAVE ABOUT HIM ('CAUSE WE'RE THE COOLEST MEN ON THE PLANET LOL). AND LOTS OF PEOPLE ASK, BUT NO, HIS NAME ISN'T A PLAY ON DR. DRE (WHO IRONICALLY IS A HIP HOP PRODUCER).

Initially, I had Lucius as a crime lord. As I developed the story I eventually decided on a mix of Kingpin, Steve Jobs and P. Diddy. I like how he's kinda lurking in the shadows right now but he's still a public figure. You'll see a lot of him in future issues.

Honestly, Mr. Fantastic didn't cross my mind at all when I came up with Mr. Flexx. I just thought a stretchy dude would be a a cool villain. He is one of the first villains I came up with so I was super excited to see Mark and Marvin bring him to life in issue 2! He'll definitely be back in a future story.

HOW WE FLIP THE SCRIPT

Page 6

Panel	Description	Dialog
6.1	A bigger panel. Rashad is flying across the lab while Mya is just standing there with her eyes glowing. Chris and Dr. Tre look shocked.	MYA MY FAULT!!!
6.2	A close up of Mya. Her eyes are back to normal and she's looking surprised.	MYA Rashad! I'm so sorry! I didn't mean too... I gotta go!
6.3	Small panel. Mya is running off crying.	
6.4	Chris is helping Rashad get up.	CHRIS You really gotta learn how to shut up sometimes.
6.5	A close up of Rashad rubbing his head.	RASHAD Lesson learned. Trust me!

Panel	Description	Dialog
13.1	An establishing shot of Dr. Tre's house.	
13.2	Mya (wearing her training uniform) and Dr. Tre (wearing his lab coat with a green button down shirt and jeans) are walking into the lab together.	DR. TRE Today we're gonna run a few exercises and then test your newest ability. MYA If I can get it to work...
13.3	Mya is flying in the air with her eyes glowing. Drones are around her.	
13.4	Mya is shooting a psionic blast at the drones.	
13.5	Mya is flying and has a force field up while a couple of drones are shooting lasers.	

K-SWAG

NAME: Rashad Carter

POWER/ABILITY: Super speed; can generate and control fire

Being a superhero was the furthest thing away from 16 year old Rashad Carter's mind. A star basketball player at Daniel Hale Williams High School, Rashad's superhero journey began when his iPod was taken by his science teacher, Dr. Tre. After school, Rashad came back to the class with his cousin Chris to get his iPod and while waiting decided to play one on one. This led to them accidently spilling chemicals that got all over them and a few days later, they were granted powers. With super speed, fire, and the name K-Swag, Rashad is the leader of Swag Patrol. While he can be stubborn, impulsive and cocky, it's those same qualities and his desire to help others that make him a leader.

MINDSET

NAME: Mya Carter

POWER/ABILITY: Flight; Force fields; Psionic energy blast; Telepathy; Telekinesis

Mya Carter is Rashad's 15 year old little sister who you could call a bookworm. Shy and to herself, she's very studious and is Dr. Tre's teacher assistant. She was helping him after school when her brother and cousin came in and caused the accident that gave her powers. She chose the name Mindset and tries to be the voice of reason but often times ends up just arguing with her big brother. Her powers are helping her come out of her shell and blossom into a young woman. Much to the dismay of Rashad and Chris, she's also starting to get noticed by the guys at school. Mya is a fast learner with the superhero adjustment but there's a lot more to her powers than even she is aware of.

Art by Leonardo Giron

BLAZE

NAME: Chris Lowery

POWER/ABILITY: Super strength; can shoot blast of concussive energy

Chris may be the tank of the group but he is a gentle giant with a heart of gold. He lives with his aunt and cousins due to his parents wanting him to have a normal life while they travel the world as doctors. Needless to say, his life has been far from normal since he went with Rashad to get his iPod. Aside from his superhero gig as Blaze, Chris enjoys playing football for his school but sometimes struggles with controlling his strength on the field. Chris also plays the unfortunate role of referee between Mya and Rashad on occasion. Overall, he considers his cousins like his own siblings and loves to remind Rashad that he's older than him by 6 weeks.

DR. TRE

NAME: Elijah "Tre" Latimer III

POWER/ABILITY: Genius level intellect; extensive knowledge in various fields of science; specializes in mechanical engineering

Dr. Tre was born in Kongo City and at a young age was considered to be one of the city's brightest and most promising minds. Graduating college at 20, he was enlisted into the US military as a mechanical engineer. He was eventually discharged however when he withheld a few of his ideas and blueprints. After that, he got involved with the organization A.R.M (Advanced Robotic Machinery) but is trying his best to part ways. He now resides in Kongo City as a science teacher at DHW High School where he met Rashad, Mya and Chris. When they came into contact with the chemicals in his room, he helped them become Swag Patrol and now aids them from his lab on missions. He's a mentor and father figure who cares for the teens and hopes his past doesn't come back to haunt them.

Art by Leonardo Giron

LUCIUS JACKSON

NAME: Lucius Jackson

POWER/ABILITY: Genius level intellect; background in technology and applied sciences; street savvy

Raised in the streets of Kongo City, Lucius Jackson turned to petty crime to help his parents and little brother. Despite his delinquency, he was a very intelligent kid graduating top of his class and receiving a full ride scholarship to college. After college he used his street smarts and genius to create Jackson Consolidated, Inc. which is one of the top technology companies in the world. Lucius is a very charismatic and charming public figure with an unquenchable thirst for power and a heavy hand in Kongo City's underworld. He has a desire and plan to rule the world one day through technology. Being a man with unlimited resources, he'll stop at nothing to reach that goal.

Art by Leonardo Giron

MR. FLEXX

NAME: Rick Fletcher

POWER/ABILITY: Can stretch his body; gun shoots a sticky substance that bounds it's target

An employee at Harold's Candy, Rick Fletcher was a scientist in charge of creating the formulas for the varieties of candy made. With a background in biology and medicine, Rick wanted to use the properties of taffy to help the body heal faster. Once his boss found out he stole company materials, he was immediately fired without actually getting to human trials. Rick decided to test on himself and ingested the taffy which gave the side effect of being able to stretch his body as far as he wanted. With this new power, he is now a full time criminal going by the name, Mr. Flexx.

Art by Leonardo Giron

THANK YOU!

This book absolutely wouldn't be possible if it weren't for all the awesome people who donated to our kickstarter! From the bottom of my heart I truly thank you guys for helping me bring my idea to life!

A.T Nguyen
Adam DJ Thompson
Adeatoyshe Heru
AJ Wone
Andre Owens
André Theobold
Chris Buchner
Chris Dickens
Christian Johnson
Dani Dixon
DeShawn
Devon Camel
Dwann Brown
E. Brunsell
Fermin Serena Hortas
Gabriel Smith
Gina Chiles
Harpreet Miglani
Henry Barajas
Jamille Harley
Jela Oba Okpara

Jennifer Priester
Jermaine
Keegan Rinker
Keenan Baker
Keithan Jones
Kevin Clark
Kurt 'KC' Christenson
Lawrence & Michael Bell
Matthew Jones
Onaji Rouse
Patrick Bächli
Punt Press
Raymond Sanders
Robert Early
Roscoe Glinton aka Johnny Tsunami
SamplingMastersXLR8
Sebastian A. Jones
Stanley
Timi Mason
William Satterwhite